Adirondack Nightmare

A Spooky Tale in the North Country

"Then away out in the woods I heard that kind of a sound that a ghost makes when it wants to tell about something that's on its mind and can't make itself understood, and so can't rest easy in its grave, and has to go about that way every night grieving."

~Mark Twain

Adirondack
Nightmare

A Spooky Tale in the North Country

Written By: Rebecca Leonard

Illustrated By: Nick Leonard

ADIRONDACK NIGHTMARE
A Spooky Tale in the North Country

Leonard Enterprises, Inc.
240 Champlain Drive
Plattsburgh, New York 12901
adirondackbooks@aol.com, http://rebeccaleonard.com

Illustrated by Nick Leonard
Edited by Elizabeth Brush

Front Cover Photo by John Mitchell, Silver Lining Photography
http://www.silverliningphotovideo.com

First Edition

ISBN-10: 1-934383-14-7
ISBN-13: 978-1-934383-14-8

Library of Congress Control Number

2007900774

This book is loosely based on my first book, <u>Adirondack Halloween: A Spooky Tale in the North Country,</u> written in 2006.

I wasn't happy with the outcome of my first book so I decided to rewrite it, using more illustrations, more character development and adding some pretty cool recipes.

I also researched the history of the Adirondacks and made a visit to Raquette Lake. It was a blast! I learned a lot on that trip and put some of my newfound information in this book.

Peace and Enjoy,
Rebecca Leonard

To Nick and Amanda, whose lives have made mine so much fuller and exciting and fun! I love you guys.

To my husband of over 17 years, Jim, my anchor, my best friend and the funniest, wackiest man I've ever met.

And to my mother, for doing her best and for always supporting and believing in me. Even when I didn't believe in myself.

Contents

Chapter One

Remembering

My name is William Durant and it is October 31st, Halloween. As I stare out my dark window, seeing fewer costumed children and hearing less laughter than usual on Halloween, I am overcome with remorse.

I know the reason for this diminishing of Halloween: this cold, dull stillness in the night, and memories of an All Hallows Eve past begin to fill my mind with unforgettable horror.

All Hallows Eve (sometimes also called Hallows Eve) is another name for Halloween. All Hallows Eve is shortened from "All-hallow-even". It is the night before "All Hallow's Day" or "All Saints' Day", a day of festivities from a culture a very long time ago. It's sometimes believed to be the only day when spirits are willing to come in contact with the physical world.

I come back to this same place, year after year, slightly older now, hoping things will change for the better. I can't imagine they ever will. My guilt consumes me every Halloween. I feel responsible for something I did as a younger man.

Here's my tale.

Chapter Two

The Camp at Raquette Lake

It's October 30th. As I look out my camp window, I'm psyched for another day away from my home in Montreal. It's my first time away on my own! It's also almost Halloween and I'm excited to be staying at an old camp in a bay called Indian Point near Raquette Lake.

Did you know....Raquette Lake is the fourth largest lake in the Adirondacks? Over 100 years ago, steamships would bring wealthy travelers to large camps along the lake.

I'm a happy guy!!

Somehow, I was lucky enough to get permission from my parents to rent the camp. At a great price to boot! I'd worked hard all summer saving enough money to stay the week of Halloween, my favorite holiday. I was looking forward to seeing the beautiful autumn leaves in the heart of the Adirondacks, doing some hiking along the trails, canoeing parts of the lake and Marion River. I'd heard it was a great time and quite a challenge.

Wow, they sure do have
big bugs around here!!

The drafty camp was an old place but it had a nice fireplace and a large Macintosh tree which was full of crisp, ripe apples. I had already spent quite some time filling a basket with them. I couldn't wait to dig in and start munching away! A local neighbor gave me a wonderful recipe to make candied apples. My mouth began to water just thinking about them.

Carmel & Chocolate Covered
Candied Apple Recipe
is on page 22.

As an 18-year-old-man, I was eager to impress my parents with my ability to be on my own. I was as happy as could be on this windy autumn day.

Caramel & Chocolate Covered Candied Apple Recipe

•Makes 6 Servings

6 large Macintosh apples, washed and dried
6 craft sticks
1 (14 oz) package individually wrapped caramels, unwrapped
2 tablespoons milk
7 ounce chocolate candy bar, broken into pieces
2 tablespoons butter

1. Remove the stems from the apples and put the craft sticks in the tops.
2. Spread out some waxed paper.
3. Put the caramels and milk in a microwave safe bowl and microwave for about 2 minutes, stirring once. Let it cool a little bit but not too much.
4. Quickly roll each apple in the caramel sauce until it's coated. Put the apples on the waxed paper.
5. Put the chocolate bar pieces and butter in a microwave safe bowl and microwave for about a minute or until the chocoate is melted. Stir.
6. Carefully drizzle the chocolate over the apples, creating any fun design you want!

Chapter Three

The Old Man

There is a local grocery store here, Lamphere's Grocery, and I decided to take a walk over there to buy some Halloween candy. A few friendly neighbors suggested I have some on hand as there were sure to be trick-or-treaters stopping by. I was familiar with the store, as I went there the first day of camp to pick up a few supplies.

The owner of the store was a mean old man and I had tried my best to ignore him on my first visit. However, on this particular day, the weather was beautiful and I was in a

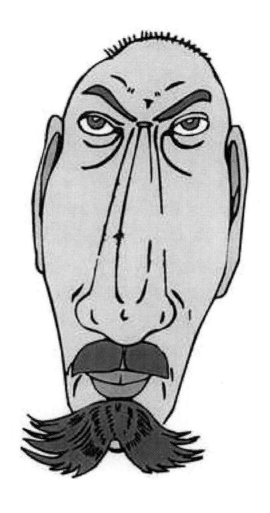

friendly mood so I aproached the ancient fellow with a casual greeting. "Morning, sir. Beautiful day today, huh?" I asked in good spirits.

"Ya want somethin'?", he croaked back. He looked up at me with his cold, red eyes.

"I, um...well...yes, sir. I was looking for some Halloween candy for the trick-or-treaters tomorrow." I felt myself begin to shrink back when he started to speak again.

"Ya come fer some candy? I ain't sold this much candy since the Halloween when the spirits came. Kinda figgers, though, people fergettin' 'bout it an' all. I ain't never gonna ferget, though, not me. I'm still lockin' up my doors an' I ain't gonna give away no candy, neither. You're a darn fool if *you* do. Just startin' somethin' up again."

The old man's angry voice with his funny North Country accent faded away, leaving me with a confused head and a lot of questions.

"Halloween when the spirits came? You mean to tell me that you actually *saw* spirits on Halloween?" I asked disbelievingly. I tried very hard to stifle a laugh which was ready to burst out of me at any second.

"What's your name, boy?" Mr. Lamphere asked with a frown on his face.

"My name is William Durant. I'm visiting for the week down from Montreal."

"William Durant?" he asked. "Are you any relation to William West Durant?"

"I don't think so. Who's he?" I was curious.

"He's probably the most famous man in all these here parts. He built up the first "Great Camp" upta Raquette Lake in the 1800's. Some o' his camps are now listed as National Landmarks," the old man explained, trying to be patient.

"What's a 'Great Camp'?" I asked.

"Well, it's a certain type o' camp, very rustic an' unique with lots o' logs

an' twigs an' natural stone. I bet yous
guys are gonna see one or two whilst
yous here. If you're lucky, that is...not
many of 'em left," he said sternly.

"Why's that?" I was almost afraid
to ask, the old man seemed to be
getting upset.

"Just *listen* to me boy! There's
a lot of history in these parts and a
lot of great people buried here. I'm
warnin' you. Don't you go near the
cemetery an' start gettin' them dead

folks mad 'cause they'll protect this
land and somethin' terrible will happen
again. Just like before." He crossed his
arms, turned his hunched back to me
and began to walk away, angrily.

"Cemetery? What cemetery? What
are you talking about? What can dead
people do? They're buried, for crying
out loud!" I couldn't help but laugh at
the cranky old dude. I was pretty sure
that spirits didn't exist. I'd never seen
one and I thought it was a bunch of
silly nonsense people talked about
when they had nothing better to do. I
stuck my tongue out at Mr. Lamphere
while he stomped away from me. I just
couldn't resist it!

"They'll massacre ya that's what they'll do. Go away, I'm a closin' up. Remember, yous been warned."

I was sure he was a crazy old fool. I was also nervous around him, so I quickly left his store. The next night was Halloween.

Chapter Four

Helicopter Seeds

As I was trekking along the road, I was grateful to be away from the crabby old man and was admiring the beautiful falling autumn leaves surrounding the area. It was a bit windy out and this made for a gorgeous display of foliage. Birches, oak, and maple trees scattered leaves from every color of the rainbow, or so it seemed. I picked up a large red sugar maple leaf and was admiring it's beauty when suddenly, I heard some kids giggling behind me.

Sugar maple trees can't grow in just any 'ol soil. They are a bit fussy and need a special mix of fine and course mineral soil with lots of nutrients. This soil type is called till and there's lots of it in the Adirondacks!

I turned around and there was a boy and a girl laughing and tossing some paper things up in the air. As soon as they noticed me, they stopped.

"Hey guys," I said cheerfully. "What's going on? Sure looks like fun!"

"What are you, a leaf peeper?!" the boy asked, rolling his eyes.

"Shhh, Tim, that's not nice," the girl whispered as she nudged the boy's arm.

"What's a 'leaf peeper'"? I asked.

"A 'leaf peeper' is a nickname we use to describe out-of-town folks who come to the Adirondacks in the fall to look at the foliage," the girl explained. "I'm Mandy and this is my brother, Tim," she added.

"Well, then I guess that's me!" I grinned. "I'm not at all offended by the nickname. My name's William."

"What are you guys throwing in
the air?" I asked them.

"Helicopters!" Tim was fired up.
"Check this out." He picked one of the
paper helicopters off the ground, held
it up as high as he could and let it go.
It twirled down to the ground much
like a helicopter's propellers would.

"That's so cool," I said. "Can I try it out?"

"Sure!" Mandy and Tim echoed, so I gave it a shot. Well, mine didn't fly quite as well as Tim's, but it still did okay.

"How did you think of making these?" I challenged them.

"We learned about it in school," Mandy offered. "They fly a lot like sugar maple seeds. Wanna see?"

"Yeah, that would be pretty interesting." I helped the kids look for a sugar maple seed. It didn't take long as there were tons of them on the ground.

Hey, it's a blast to press these on your nose! Try it and see!

We began throwing the seeds up in the air to see whose could twirl the best. It was such a blast, even for an 18-year old like me.

"Hey," said Tim. "We were just going to go inside for some milk and cookies. Wanna come?"

"Ah...well...um," I started, a little embarrassed because I felt I was too old for milk and cookies. Flying seeds was one thing but this was a bit much.

"Come on. Mom makes the best maple syrup cookies in the world!" pleaded Mandy.

"Sure, why not. Thanks." I gave in easily. My stomach *was* growling from hunger.

We made the short walk up to their house and I was surprised to find out that their parents ran a maple sugar house. We talked for quite some time and Mandy gave me the paper pattern to make my own helicopter seeds.

Tim and Mandy's mother, Mrs. Huntington, was a wonderful hostess and made me feel quite at home, especially when she asked me to call her Kathy. When the kids went back outside to play, we got around to talking about old man Lamphere. Kathy explained to me that Mr. Lamphere had an only child, a son, who was killed in a war. His beloved son was buried in the local cemetery and, according to Kathy, Mr. Lamphere feels very protective of that area.

"Lots of folks in the Adirondacks have experienced weird things that can't be explained," Kathy began. "One story involves a distant relative of old man Lamphere. In the 1800's, Stephen Lamphere built a house on a piece of land where it was said an old peddler was murdered. Stephen Lamphere would hear footsteps, rapping on a window, a woman's moan, the peddler's face was seen, and his wagon was heard." Kathy shuttered and looked down at her folded hands on the table.

"Wow, that's quite a tale." I didn't know what else to say. I certainly wasn't one to believe in an old wives' tale like this one.

"Well, I guess I'd better be on my way," I said to Kathy as I stood up from the table. "Thanks so much for everything."

"My pleasure, William. Take good care of yourself, enjoy the beautiful weather, and be sure to steer clear of our old cemetery, you hear?" Kathy smiled and gave me a hug.

"I'll be careful, I promise." I reassured her and was on my way with my paper helicopter pattern. I made sure I was well out of sight before I shook my head in disbelief about her story.

Kathy's Famous Maple Syrup Cookie Recipe

1 1/2 cups maple syrup
1/2 cup white sugar
1/2 cup shortening
1 tsp. baking soda
1 cup oatmeal
1/2 tsp. salt
2 cups flour

Preheat oven to 375

1. Dissolve the baking soda in a little warm water.
2. Heat the maple syrup, sugar and shortening to a boil.
3. Remove from the stove and add the baking soda.
4. Let cool.
5. When cold, add the oatmeal, salt and flour. Mix well.
6. Roll out (not too thin) and cut with a cookie cutter.
7. Bake until light brown, about 8 to 10 minutes.
8. Enjoy!

Tim & Mandy's
Helicopter Seed Pattern

Remember to copy this from the book and don't cut it out directly from the book! Yikes! Feel free to trace it or photocopy it.

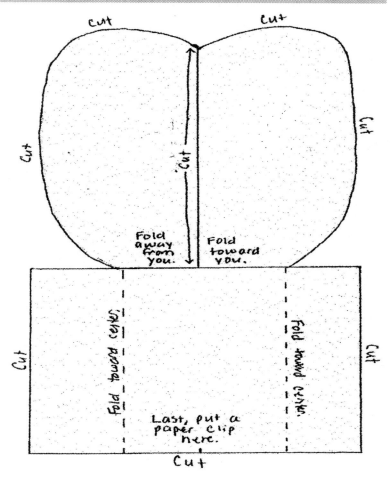

Chapter Five

John and Mary's Diner

After walking for quite a while I realized I never got any Halloween candy from old man Lamphere's store. I saw a sign for a diner up ahead and decided to get a bite to eat and to see if they sold candy there. I was getting pretty hungry again. The wind was really picking up and it was becoming damp. This was making my walk rather unpleasant, but it was well worth the chilly hike when I walked into John and Mary's Diner. I was warmly greeted by a nice couple who were behind the diner's counter. There were a few other folks sitting at tables and stools and they nodded to me with a warm welcome.

John and Mary's Diner

"Howdy sir. Set yerself right down here and I'll get you a nice cup of coffee. My name's John and this here's my wife, Mary," the jovial man said heartily.

"A cup of java sounds perfect!" I welcomed the idea enthusiastically as I rubbed my hands together to warm them up a bit. "What's your special for the day?"

"We've got the best hamburger macaroni soup and michigan platter you'll ever find in the Adirondacks," Mary answered kindly, looking into my eyes.

"I've never tried or heard of either so that sounds great. I feel adventurous today!" I welcomed the cup of coffee warming my hands.

"Never heard of a michigan? Oh dear, well you haven't lived until you've had one of ours. It's a hot dog with a special secret sauce. Kind of like a chili dog only better. The best way to order them is by saying 'michigan, with, buried'," reasoned Mary.

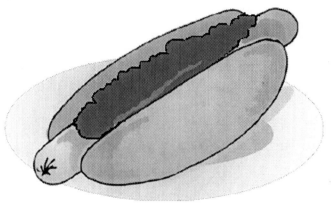

Best michigan sauce recipe
EVER is on page 56.

Most North Country natives have different memories and ideas about how the michigan came to be in the North Country but no one can seem to agree. It's still a mystery!

We never write the food "michigan" with a capital M, but we do write the state "Michigan" with a capital M because it's a state!

"I always thought Michigan was just a state! What does 'with, buried' mean?" I was a bit confused at that point.

"It means with onions, buried under the hot dog. Are you still in?" teased John.

"Absolutely!" I said, excitedly.

"Well, then, let me git your dinner started. What's your name, son?"

"William Durant, I'm from Montreal."

"Durant? You any relation to—" started John.

"—William West Durant?" I jumped in. "No, but I hear he was a famous man in these parts."

"You betcha. His whole family dedicated themselves to the Adirondacks. Ok, I'm off to start your meal." John stopped to talk with some of the other customers then went in to the kitchen.

As I sat on my stool, I looked outside at the dark, damp, cold night and shivered. I wasn't looking forward to the walk back to camp. I had my trusty flashlight with me so I knew I could find my way back.

"What's your pop do for work up in Montreal?" asked Mary as she set up my napkin and silverware.

"My family's in the lumbering business. I guess that's why I've always been interested in nature and the outdoors," I answered.

Outside, I noticed half of a bathtub with a lady in it. It looked religious, but I'd never seen one before so I asked Mary,

"What's that lawn ornament in front of your diner? It's very unique." I didn't want to admit to Mary that I didn't understand it.

"Why that's called 'Mary on the Half Shell'. Some folks also call it 'Bathtub Mary' or 'Our Lady of the Bathtub'. It's a symbol of the Virgin Mary and the tub symbolizes a grotto. Do you know what a grotto is?" Mary asked as she filled my coffee cup up again.

"I have no idea. What is it?"

"A grotto is a cave-like structure that protects The Virgin Mary."

I nodded politely. I wasn't sure if I would put one outside my house when I got older, but I was grateful for the explanation of the statue.

John placed the dinner in front of me and asked me if I had met some of the local folks. Between bites I answered, "Yes, as a matter of fact, I was talking with the old man in the grocery store—"

"—"ya mean Mr. Lamphere's place?" Mary interrupted.

"Sure, that's it. He was telling me about that Halloween long ago when the so-called 'spirits' came." I laughed. "I think he's a bit crazy."

"No, William, he ain't crazy. A little bit scared maybe, but not crazy. Ya see, a few years ago, we had a new fella visitin' in town. He came in from New York City to help with some engineering plans for this area. Nice guy: don't recall his name, but he sure caused us a lot of trouble.

"For some reason, on Halloween, he went runnin' an' screamin' through the cemetery. I reckon he got spooked by a spirit or somethin'," John continued.

"Anyhow, he got all the spirits riled up and the spirits took him away. Some folks say they massacred the New York city guy."

"All I know for sure is that no one ever saw him again. That night, the spirits started to scare every Halloweening kid in town. Poor kids, they were frightened out of their skins. Though it seems like the last few years people have been going out for treats more and more. I guess they're forget- tin' 'bout it now. It's time we got our Halloween back." John looked at me with sad eyes.

"Well, I don't believe in ghosts or spirits or anything of the kind," I declared. "I think it's just nonsense. No offense to anyone in Indian Point!"

"Son, you sure do have a lot to learn about these Adirondacks," John said. "There's been lots of sightings of ghosts and spirits all over the place. The history of the area says it all. Native Americans were slaughtered here, the French and Indian War saw lots of soldiers killed. Why, there's still sightings going on over at Fort Ticonderoga to this day!

"I wouldn't be one to jump to any conclusions about this. I've had a sighting myself in the old cemetery which still makes my skin crawl every time I think of it." John sounded nervous.

I wanted to change the subject so I said, "I also met a nice family over at the maple sugar house. Kathy shared some of her delicious maple sugar cookies and they were awesome!" I stood up to pay my bill. I'd had enough of this wacky talk. I didn't want to hear John's ghost story. I told John and Mary I had to head back to camp before it got too late.

"Well, have a safe trip back to camp, dear, and be careful. Remember to stay away from that cemetery, ya hear?" Mary warned softly.

"Sure, you bet. Hey, I almost forgot. Do you guys sell Halloween candy?" I asked.

"Sorry, son; we don't carry any candy." John replied.

Disappointed, I said goodbye before John continued with his ghost story. I'd had 3 cups of coffee during our visit and was getting a bit antsy.

About 8:30p.m. I started heading back
to the old camp.

John and Mary's Best Michigan Sauce Recipe EVER!

16 oz tomato sauce
1 lb ground meat (beef, venison)
3/4 tsp garlic powder
2 tsp chili powder
1 tsp cumin
1 tsp pepper
1 tsp salt
1/4 cup hot sauce (or to taste)

Ok, now how easy is this? Put all of these ingredients into a saucepan together. You don't need to brown the meat at all! Let it simmer, stirring it once in a while, until it's the thickness you desire.

By the way, don't forget to bury the onions, enjoy!

Chapter Six

Walking Back to Camp

While walking in the dark with my trusty flashlight, an idea struck me. Why not take a stroll through the cemetery? I had a lot of energy from the coffee and was ready for a little thrill. Because of the warm dinner inside my belly, the cold dampness of the night didn't seem to disturb me one bit.

The haunting cry of the loons in the background further inspired me for the journey.

The mournful cry of the loon reminds some people of a sick, demented person. Thus, the phrase "crazy as a loon" was invented.

Loons like to eat fresh water fish and need large areas of open water to take off because they're such heavy birds. They're taken with the Adirondacks because the mountains in this region boast many large lakes.

Chapter Seven

The Cemetery

On the way back to camp, I came upon the old, rusty iron cemetery gates. They creaked and groaned against the wind when I pushed them open. A weedy stone road was barely visible in the darkening night. I turned on my flashlight to follow it.

As I started down the old path, a strange feeling overwhelmed me. The air seemed thicker, more dense than normal. My breathing began to come in long, hard gasps. My pulse began racing. As I looked at my surroundings, a piercing chill crept up my spine.

With my flashlight I saw this was a strange cemetery. The trees were barren. The grass was not quite green. The fallen leaves were black and rotted. All of the gravestones were cracked and gray and unusually depressing.

"Why am I scared?" I asked myself out loud. "There are no such things as or ghosts or demons. So what's the big deal?"

To prove to myself and to the gloomy cemetery I wasn't scared, I began to shout,

"Come over here you stupid ghosts! Come on. Are you afraid of an outsider coming into your depressing backyard? I'm not afraid of something that isn't even here!" By then I was enjoying myself so I continued.

"What? Are you afraid of an 18-year-old man? You're all a bunch of nothings. Come out now, I dare you!" I was angry at the whole scene.

"I won't waste any more of my time on you!" I yelled and started to walk away, flustered. I took one last look around the graveyard.

"Hello?" Was someone calling my name?

Turning toward the sound, I screamed when I saw a horrifying and repulsive looking spirit standing beside one of the moldy gravestones.

Chapter Eight

Spirits?

Looking closer, I noticed the spirit was growing brighter and brighter and taller and taller. Suddenly, it burst into flames. Then another flaming spirit appeared, and another and another! The large and disfigured spirits had human features. Standing about seven-feet tall, they towered over all the gravestones. There were many of them, too many to count. I didn't move right away. I began to think. This is some silly childish Halloween prank. After all, John told me the local children were just getting back into the Halloween spirit.

Suddenly, in the distance, I heard the disembodied scream of a man. At the same time, my flashlight went out! I couldn't believe it! I banged it against a gravestone thinking the batteries were loose but it simply stopped working!

I had put in new batteries the first day of camp. I was about to find out that this was no malicious childish trick.

Stomp. Stomp. Stomp.

"William! William! William Durant!" I heard someone call my name in the distance.

"W-w-ho's th-th-there"? My voice cracked with fear. I turned toward the sound, every nerve in my body shaking.

No, this was no trick. Indeed, it was far too real. The creatures did not speak, nor did they utter a sound.

"Who called my name?" I croaked. The disfigured spirits began to creep in closer and closer to me.

Suddenly, one of the creatures reached his long, witchlike claw out to me. It was clammy and mutilated. I turned to try to find some sort of escape but it was hopeless. I was trapped. Before I knew what had happened, they were upon me, scratching at my face, neck and chest. I screamed.

All of a sudden, my flashlight began working again! The creatures moaned and immediately retreated back to wherever they came. They did this in a flash, almost too fast to see. I was overwhelmed. I was tired. I had scratches on my body that I couldn't explain. I wanted desperately to go back to camp. I had never been that tired or so exhausted in my life.

"William? Is that you, boy?" I became dizzy and started swaying as I began to faint on the dirty and clammy cemetery ground.

Chapter Nine

Camp, Please

I awoke to someone, or something, vigorously shaking my shoulders. I looked around. I wasn't in the cemetery anymore.

"William, wake up!"

The stench of dry, hard blood on my body overwhelmed me. I had scratches on my face, neck, arms, seemingly on every inch of me. I felt weak and dizzy. I slowly rose from the ground and looked up, dazed and confused. Old man Lamphere was there, sizing me up.

"You allright, boy?" He asked, agitated.

"Yeah...no...I don't know," I stammered, still confused. "What happened? Where am I?"

"Well, sure looks ta me like ya decided ta come 'round the cemetery after all 'n create quite a stir," the old man answered. "We're at my store now. You're safe, boy."

"At your store? I was in the cemetery when—"

"—when the spirits attacked ya. I know. I was there. When I saw ya faint I carried ya back ta my place and cleaned ya up a bit," he finished, shaking his head.

"So it's true about the spirits. I can't believe I didn't listen to everyone. Was that you calling my name in the cemetery?" I asked.

"Ya, 'twas me. Who else warned ya?" The old man was still shaking his head, disapprovingly.

"Well, altogether there were three people...you, Mary from the diner and Kathy from the maple sugar house," I answered, sheepishly. "Why were you in the cemetery?"

"I was a visitin' my son," Mr. Lamphere's voice became a whisper.

At that point I didn't know what to say to the old man. I felt sorry for him. I knew he was in pain over the loss of his son. But, he went on...

"Boy, the spirits there don't want to harm ya. Why they's just protectin' their honor and their place o' rest. They didn't know ya so they attacked ya when ya provoked 'em. I heard ya yellin' at the poor ol' souls. Ya shoulda jus' let them be." He finished angrily.

"You're right, Mr. Lamphere. I'm so ashamed for not listening to your advice. I'm so very sorry," I sighed.

The old man said, "I think your flashlight protected ya, boy. Light is a symbol of mercy to them. When they felt ya really wasn't a bad fella, they gave ya your light back and letcha be."

"What can I do to fix this?" I asked. "I want to make this right, I feel terrible about my foolishness."

"Boy, I honestly don't know. The spirits will be forgiving. Just ya give 'em some time," he said. "Now, let's git ya back to camp so as you can git some rest."

We slowly made our way back to camp. We saw no trick-or-treaters, no lights on in houses, no cars on the road. I knew then that I had ruined this Halloween for the good folks at Indian Point Bay. I apologized again to the old man and we said our goodbyes.

I went inside and locked my door. I was exhausted. I couldn't make it to my bed in the other room. Instead, I fell asleep at my desk, 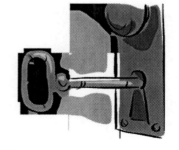 which was closest to the door.

Chapter Ten

Going Home

H orrible nightmares of spirits and graveyards filled my dreams.

When I woke up, I packed my bags to head home to Montreal. I kept asking myself, 'What can I do? How can I fix this? There must be a way.'

It was then and there that I vowed to myself, to Mr. Lamphere, to John and Mary, to Kathy and to Mandy and Tim that I would find a way to let this wonderful community have its Halloween back.

I would return someday and bring All Hallows Eve back to Indian Point Bay and to Raquette Lake. I would learn to forgive myself for my mistake and I would make up for it. I just needed some time to think.

Nobody deserves to be helped who don't try to help himself.
and "faith without works" is a risky doctrine.

~Mark Twain

Bibliography

Online Sources

"Adirondack Great Camps." *Great Camps of the Adirondacks history & slide show, pie irons, fireside recipes.* Retrieved 12 Jan 2007. http://www.greatcamps.com.

"Halloween." *Wikipedia, The free encyclopedia.* Retrieved 10 Jan 2007. http://en.wikipedia.org/wiki/Halloween.

"Mark Twain Quotes." *Mark Twain quotations.* Retreived 24 Jan 2007. http://www.twainquotes.com.

"Michigan Gordie Little." *All Points North-Michigans-A North Country Custom.* Retrieved 20 Jan 2007. http://www.apnmag.com/spring_2005/michiganhistory.htm

"William Durant Great Camps." *History of Adirondack Architecture.* Retrieved 12 Jan 2007.

Bibliography

Books

Jenkins, Jerry, and Andy Keal.
The Adirondack Atlas. Bronx, NY: Wildlife
Conservation Society, 2004.

Revai, Cheri. *Weird Northern New York*.
Utica, NY: North Country Books, Inc, 2006

Storey, Mike. *Why the Adirondacks Look
the way They do. A Natural History*.
Self-Published by Mike Storey, 2006.

Tekiela, Stan. *Birds of New York Field
Guide - Second Edition*. Cambridge, MN:
Adventure Publications, 2005

About the Author

Photograph by Jim Leonard

Rebecca (Becky) Leonard is a longtime resident of Plattsburgh, New York, living just north of the Adirondack Park. She spends many hours boating on Lake Champlain with her family and friends and enjoys knitting at their camp in Champlain, New York. She is married to Jim and they have two wonderful children, Nick and Amanda, and a houseful of pets. She is busy working on the sequel to this book, along with several other book projects.

Author Acknowledgments

I'd like to thank my mother, Beth Brush, from the bottom of my heart for her editing expertise and encouragement. You've always been such a great role model, Mom.

I also want to convey sincere thanks to the following for their contributions to the book's storyline:

Jim Leonard	Amanda Leonard
Nick Leonard	John Mitchell
Kurt Reh	Victoria Herkalo
Joe Brush	Gordie Little
Sid Couchey	Gerrie Leonard

A big thanks to Kurt Reh, Victoria Herkalo and Nick Leonard for helping me wrap up the ending of the story. Thanks for the flaslight idea, Kurt! Thanks to Marie McGrath for the delicious maple sugar cookie recipe. Thanks to Amy Brush and Jim Leonard for insisting I put in the "maple seed on the nose" idea. You guys are right, it's a blast to do! Victoria, thanks for telling me I should be a writer. The look on your face when you read my original manuscript from 1978 said it all. I owe you a big one.

Last, but absolutely not least, I'd like to thank Harold Brohinsky. Harold, your encouragment and words of wisdom have changed me forever and I can never thank you enough. I love you.

LEONARD ENTERPRISES, INC.
240 Champlain Drive
Plattsburgh, New York 12901
adirondackbooks@aol.com

QUICK ORDER FORM

EMAIL ORDERS:
adirondackbooks@aol.com or visit
www.rebeccaleonard.com

FAX ORDERS: SEND THIS FORM.
518-561-2443

POSTAL ORDERS: MAIL TO:
Leonard Enterprises, Inc.
240 Champlain Drive
Plattsburgh, New York 12901
Include check or money order.

TELEPHONE ORDERS:
518-561-2443 Have credit card ready.

Please send me _____ copies of Adirondack Nightmare
at $9.95 per copy (NYS residents include 7.75% for
books shipped to New York State addresses).

Name:_____

Address: _____

City:_____ State _____ Zip _____

Telephone: _____

Email Address: _____

Shipping: $3 for first book and $2 for each additional.

Printed in the United States
74024LV00002B/328-999